Disney's Christmas Storybook

DISNEY PRESS

New York

TABLE OF CONTENTS

TABLE OF CONTENTS

Written by Elizabeth Spurr

Interior design by Alfred Giuliani

Artwork for the following stories was created by DRI Artworks: *101 Dalmatians: A Christmas For-Giving*; *Cinderella: A Merry Christmas for Mice*; *Oliver and Company: Christmas Is for Friends*; *The Little Mermaid: Ariel's Christmas Under the Sea*; *The Aristocats: An Aristocat-ic Christmas*; *Bambi: The Wonderful Winter Tree*; *Dumbo: The Best Christmas*; and *Beauty and the Beast: The Enchanted Christmas*. Pencil sketches for *A Bug's Life: Flik's Christmas Invention* by Gita Lloyd, paintings by Eric Binder. Artwork for *Lady and the Tramp: Lady's Christmas Surprise* by Francesc Mateu. Pencil sketches for *Pinocchio: Pinocchio's Perfect Gift* by Orlando de la Paz, paintings by Eric Binder. Artwork for *Winnie the Pooh: Pooh's Jingle Bells* by Josie Yee. Pencil sketches for *The Hunchback of Notre Dame: Christmas in the Bell Tower* by Mark Marderosian, paintings by Eva Lopez. Artwork for *Tarzan: Christmas in the Jungle* by Jose Maria Cardona. Artwork for *Robin Hood: Christmas for Everyone* by Barcelona Studio. Pencil sketches for *Snow White: A Christmas to Remember* by Fernando Guell, paintings by Fred Marvin. Pencil sketches for *Toy Story: Andy's Christmas Puppy* by Mark Marderosian, paintings by Tom La Padula.

101 Dalmatians is based on the book *The One Hundred and One Dalmatians* by Dodie Smith, published by Viking Press.
Bambi is based on the book *Bambi, A Life in the Woods* by Felix Salten, published by Simon & Schuster.
Dumbo is suggested by the story *Dumbo, the Flying Elephant*, by Helen Aberson and Harold Perl. Copyright © 1939 by Rollabook Publishers, Inc.
A Bug's Life © Disney Enterprises, Inc./Pixar Animation Studios.
Winnie the Pooh is based on the Pooh stories by A. A. Milne (Copyright the Pooh Properties Trust).
TARZAN® Owned by Edgar Rice Burroughs, Inc. and Used by Permission. Copyright © 1999 Edgar Rice Burroughs, Inc. and Disney Enterprises, Inc. All rights reserved.
Toy Story © Disney Enterprises, Inc./Pixar Animation Studios. Mr. Potato Head® and Mrs. Potato Head® are registered trademarks of Hasbro, Inc. Used with Permission. © Hasbro, Inc. All rights reserved.

First Edition

3 5 7 9 10 8 6 4 2

This book is set in 20-point Cochin.

Library of Congress Catalog Card Number: 99-68121

ISBN: 0-7868-3260-6

For more Disney Press fun, visit www.disneybooks.com

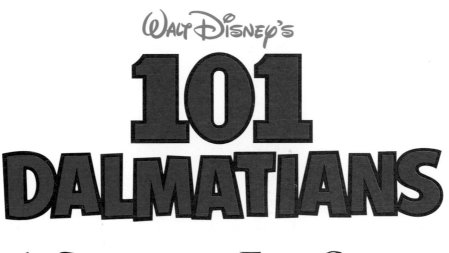

Walt Disney's
101 DALMATIANS

A CHRISTMAS FOR-GIVING

One winter evening as Pongo and Perdita watched TV with their 99 puppies, Roger and Nanny hauled a huge tree into the parlor. It was fresh and green and made the room smell like a pine forest.

Once Nanny and Roger had gone, the puppies went to take a closer look. "What's going on?" The puppies turned to their mother, looking slightly alarmed.

"Don't worry, dears," said Perdy. "This is just the beginning of Christmas."

"Christ-mess? Christ-muss?"

It was both mess and muss. That night the floor was covered with pine needles, boxes of ornaments, tinsel garlands, and strings of twinkling lights. There was

barely space for the puppies to sit.

Roger and Anita began acting very strangely,

climbing on stepladders, hanging shiny colored balls on

the tree limbs, and arguing about the tree top: should it

have a star, or an angel?

At last the tree was finished, and the room tidied. When Roger pressed a switch, the lights and shiny ornaments cast a magical glow about the room. The puppies gawked wide-eyed at the tree. This Christmas business must be something very special, they thought.

That night, when Pongo and Perdita tucked the

puppies into their baskets, they explained about the fuss and muss of Christmas. It was a time when two-legged creatures like Roger and Anita tried to show their families and friends how much they cared for them.

People sent cards and
baked cookies and fruitcakes.
They sang carols and hung
mistletoe so they would have
an excuse to kiss and hug.

It was all very strange, but,
Pongo assured the puppies, they would grow to love
Christmas, especially the beef bones left over from
dinner.

"And that's not all," added Perdy. "On Christmas
Eve, after everyone's in bed, people sneak presents

under the tree for those they love."

"Because," said Pongo, "Christmas is about giving."

"Will we get presents?" asked Rolly.

"Maybe," Perdy replied.

"I remember Anita gave me a new collar last year."

"And I got a red ball," said Pongo.

"I hope someone loves us," said Penny.

"Don't worry," said Perdy. "You are loved."

On Christmas morning the puppies woke at dawn. They crept into the living room. Sure enough, there were piles of brightly wrapped packages under the tree.

"We are loved!" said Freckles. They all dove into the pile, tossing and ripping and tearing. *Rrrrmph!* Unwrapping was so fun!

Lucky pulled open a box. His jaw dropped. "Perfume?"

Penny dragged a spotted necktie from the tissue. "Now, what do I need with more spots?"

Freckles, looking downcast, held up a lace handkerchief.

And when Patch nosed out a satin nightgown, Lucky said, "Uh-oh!"

And the rest of the puppies chorused, "Uh-oh!"

Just then they heard Roger's and Anita's voices in

the hallway.

"Out of here!"

said Rolly. All 99

scampered,

hiding behind

sofas, under

chairs, or in the

folds of the curtains.

They heard Roger's footsteps cross the threshold.

"What on earth?"

Anita said, "Oh, dear!"

Roger called, "Perdy, Pongo. Where are you?"

The puppies heard the tick of their parents' claws as they scurried toward the parlor. When they came into the room, Pongo said, "Woof!"

And Perdy repeated, "Woof!"

In their hiding places, the puppies trembled. They were in for it now.

Then, like music, came
Anita's peal of laughter.

And Roger said, with a
chuckle, "Looks like we had
some help opening our gifts."

After a pause Anita said,
"Wasn't that kind of the
puppies!"

"Let's call them," said
Roger, "and say thanks. Here,
puppies. Come here, pups!"

The puppies looked at one another. Should they answer?

Anita said in a loud voice, "There are still so many boxes to unwrap. I do wish they'd come and help."

One by one the puppies came into view, first creeping, then bounding. *Yip, yip, yip!*

They gathered around the tree as Roger pulled packages from under the branches. "Go for it, boys and girls!"

With happy squeals the puppies tore into the bright wrappings—the tangled ribbon, the crunchy cardboard, the crinkly papers. Pongo and Perdy looked at each other. "Shall we join them?" whispered Pongo.

"This is their first Christmas," replied Perdy. "Let *them* have the fun."

They both looked on with longing as a snowstorm of tissue flew through the air.

When all the gifts had been opened and piled neatly and all the papers set ablaze in the fireplace, Anita

brought out a large basket. "Sorry we didn't have time to wrap these," she said. "But then"—she smiled—"maybe you've done enough work for today."

She handed each puppy a squeaky toy. From the

bottom of the basket she drew two red-and-green Christmas sweaters for Pongo and Perdy. "Anita knitted them herself," said Roger.

When the Christmas feasting was finally over and the last rib bone chewed, Perdy tucked the pups into

their baskets. "We like

Christmas!" said Pepper. "We

like our toys!" said Rolly. "We

like tissue paper!" said Patch.

"Remember I told you that

Christmas was about giving?" asked Perdy.

"We remember," said the puppies.

"It's also about *for*-giving," said Pongo gently. "You

were lucky that Roger and Anita had the Christmas

spirit."

The puppies looked at him, puzzled.

"From now on there will be no more unwrapping—unless you have permission. Can you remember that?"

And they did remember.

At least, until Christmas came again.

Walt Disney's

Cinderella

A MERRY CHRISTMAS FOR MICE

It was Christmas Eve, and Cinderella was lonely. Cinderella's stepmother and her two daughters, Drizella and Anastasia, had driven off to spend the

holiday in the country with their wealthy cousins. Cinderella had not been invited. She was left at home to sweep and scrub and feed the animals.

As Cinderella sat

by the extinguished fire, thoughts of past Christmases
flooded over her—how she and her father had loved
decorating their home and wrapping gifts for the many
friends who came to
visit. A tear rolled
down her cheek.

Gus and Jaq
skittered to her side.
Her mouse friends
seemed to sense when
she was in need.

"Cinderelly sad?" asked Jaq.

Cinderella put her head in her hands. "It's just that . . . it's Christmas Eve!" she said.

"Crismusseve, Cinderelly?" chittered Gus. "Doesn't look like Crismusseve."

"Where the holly?" asked Jaq. "Where the tree? What kinda Crismuss can *this* be?"

Cinderella explained that her stepmother and

stepsisters had decided that, since they were going

away, Christmas would make too much of a mess.

"I love the Christmas mess," sighed Cinderella,

"and the busy-ness. That's all part of the fun."

"Not too late," said Gus. "Let's *us* get busy,

Cinderelly!"

Cinderella, with a large bowl of milk, lured Lucifer the cat into a small room upstairs and locked the door.

Then Gus and Jaq called the other mice and birds into action. From the nearby forest they brought pine boughs, holly branches, and mistletoe, which they wove into lush garlands.

Meanwhile, Cinderella found and cut a small but well-shaped tree, which her dog, Bruno, hauled home on a sled. She and her friends hung red apples and colorful strings of berries on the boughs. Finally,

she trimmed the branches with household candles.

When the tree was lit, Cinderella and her friends stood back to admire it. She shivered with delight. "A Christmas tree is a sign of hope," she said. "I feel more hopeful already."

"Me hopeful, too," said

Gus. "We gonna eat good

Christmas dinner?"

"Oh, dear," sighed

Cinderella. "With all the

bustle, I forgot. You all must

be hungry."

She scanned the cupboards,

which were almost bare. With

a lock on the cellar store of

hams, cheeses, and preserves,

there was little to be had,

except an oat cake and a pot of yesterday's pea soup.

Cinderella put the poor dinner on the table. "I'm sorry I can't offer a feast," she said.

"Whole oat cake?" said Gus. "That feast. Better than crumbs, yes?"

"Feast not just food," Jaq told her, "but friends. Agree, Cinderelly?"

And soon, amid much gaiety, the last crumb disappeared.

After dinner Cinderella picked more apples from the garden tree and made a deep-dish pie.

As spicy aromas drifted through the rooms, it did seem like Christmas after all. Never mind the past or the future. She was warm and fed and among caring

friends. "Thank you for sharing my Christmas," she said.

"Waitee, waitee, Cinderelly!" said Jaq, with a wide grin.

"Gotta open giftee," said Gus. From behind his back he drew a small package, wrapped in crumpled paper.

Cinderella opened it. "How beautiful!" From some of Drizella's cast-off ribbons, the mice had woven a tiara, which sparkled with tiny beads. When she put it on, the mice exclaimed, "A princess! A princess!"

"You're *our* princess," said Jaq.

Cinderella looked down at her adoring friends. "You have been so good to me," she said. "I wish I had a gift for you."

"You save us from Lucifee!" said Gus. "That *big* giftee."

At that moment they heard a yowl from upstairs.

"Lucifer!" Up to this moment Cinderella had forgotten

him. It didn't seem fair to

make the cat sit alone in a

cold room while the others

celebrated Christmas.

"Would you mind if I

brought him to join us?"

"Lucifee?" The mice

scampered.

Jaq shuddered. "We'll be feastie for that beastie!"

"Couldn't you all declare a truce?" asked Cinderella.
"At least for Christmas Eve?"

Gus hesitated, then sighed, "If *he* will, *we* will."

Cinderella dashed upstairs. "I'm sorry, Lucifer. I'd

let you join the party, but we're all afraid you'd like a mouse for Christmas dinner."

Lucifer shook his head hard. Then he patted his belly, and pointed to the empty milk bowl.

"Promise?"

Lucifer nodded.

And so it came to pass that, on the day that, by tradition, the lion lies down with

the lamb, Lucifer snoozed contentedly by the fire,
while Cinderella and her mouse friends spent a peaceful
evening—sharing their apple pie.

Disney's Oliver & Company

CHRISTMAS IS FOR FRIENDS

A heavy snow fell outside Jenny's Fifth Avenue town house, but inside, a blazing fire warmed the luxurious living room. "Look, Oliver," sang Jenny,

"we're going to have a white Christmas!"

Oliver looked up sadly from his cushion by the hearth.

Jenny sat on the hearth next to him.

"What's the matter,

kitty? Don't you feel well?"

Oliver let Jenny pet him and scratch under his chin. But soon he settled back onto his cushion.

"I know what's the matter," said Jenny as she reached for a photograph. "You miss your friends."

Although they had promised to visit often, Oliver's friends from the barge, Dodger, Einstein,

Tito, and the rest, had not been around in a while.

Oliver knew they were probably busy helping Fagin

make a living. So Oliver's only animal company came

from Jenny's poodle, Georgette, who, although friendly

of late, was too snooty to be much fun.

I know what I'll do, thought Jenny. I'll throw Oliver a Christmas party. That will cheer him up.

Her parents were staying with relatives in Europe for the Christmas holiday. With no one around but the servants, Jenny could use some company herself.

With the help of Winston, she wrote an invitation to

Fagin and the rest of Oliver's friends. Winston printed it with fancy curlicues on a parchment scroll.

To Messrs. and Mme.
Fagin, Dodger, Rita, Einstein,
Francis, and Tito:
The pleasure of your company
is requested for dinner
on Christmas Eve, December 24,
at six o'clock in the evening.
R.S.V.P. Black tie optional.

Winston tied the invitation with a gold ribbon and delivered it to the barge. He found no one at home, so he tied it to the doorknob.

Fagin was delighted with the invitation and read it to his friends, who leaped and yipped at the news.

"I bet that'll be some feed," said Fagin. "I think I can scrape up a black tie for each of us. But I wonder, where in town can we find an R.S.V.P.?"

Jenny, Winston, and the staff set about preparing a

magnificent Christmas Eve dinner—roast beef, roast duckling, roast goose, and lots of puddings and pies.

Winston called in the florist, who draped the

walls and the staircases with garlands of holly, all

ablaze with white twinkling lights. Then they erected

an enormous Christmas tree, hung with gold and silver

balls, and delicious

dog bones around

the bottom.

Jenny went

through dozens of

department stores,

shopping for gifts

for the Christmas

Eve guests. Oliver was delighted to see Jenny returning to the car with her arms overflowing with gifts. The thought of seeing his old friends made Oliver very happy.

On Christmas Eve, everything was ready. "I hope they'll come," said Jenny, looking a little worried. "They didn't R.S.V.P."

At that moment, six o'clock on the dot, the bell rang.
Winston opened the door and there were the six
friends, each wearing a black tie. Oliver was beside

himself with joy.
Oliver and the
dogs, unable to
contain their
excitement, chased
one another around
the room.

All the guests

enjoyed the elegant dinner. Little was left but a pile of

bones, which the cook scraped into one enormous

doggy bag. Afterward, Jenny sat everyone around the

tree, and handed out her gifts: a handsome pocket

watch for Fagin, a sausage string for Dodger, and a

small wicker basket with a lid for Tito to put his

tools in. Francis opened a videotape of Shakespeare's plays and Einstein received a comfy pillow for his bed. Rita and Georgette opened their packages and were overjoyed to receive beautiful handmade sweaters.

Oliver received a tiny, diamond-studded bell, which

jingled when Jenny hung it on his collar. "That way I'll always know where you are," she said. Georgette, in her new angora sweater, looked slightly miffed but said

nothing.

"And now, Jenny," said Fagin, "it's our turn." He laid out six crumpled packages tied with butcher string. "I'm sorry we couldn't find an R.S.V.P.," he said. "We looked everywhere."

Jenny tried not to giggle. Then she opened the first package. "How nice!" she exclaimed. Her friends had gone to a lot of trouble to give her a cuckoo clock with an exquisite bird but no chime, a beautiful book of fairy tales with a taped cover, a picture frame with no glass, a one-armed doll who had beautiful eyes, a string of beads with no clasp, and a satin purse with a hole in it.

"How lovely," she said, and she meant it.

"'Twasn't much." Fagin looked down at his scuffed shoes. "We found them all in the Dumpster. I didn't figure you'd spend so much on all of us."

"Christmas isn't a spending contest," laughed Jenny. "I love all my gifts. They're all so unique. And I do love . . ." She got no further, because *Pffft!* with a crackling blue flash, every light in the house went out!

"Speaking of surprises," said Fagin. "All these

Christmas lights have blown a fuse."

"I'll try to find a flashlight," said Jenny. As she groped her way across the marble floors, *Thummmp!* she bumped into a table that held one of her mother's prized vases. "Whoa!" she said as she fell to the floor.

"Are you hurt?" called Fagin through the darkness.

"I . . . I don't think so!" she said.

"Don't move Jenny," said Winston. "There may be broken shards around you."

While Fagin and Winston tried to find Jenny, Tito, the electrical wizard, sniffed out the faulty fuse, and within minutes the room was once again aglow.

"I'm all right," said Jenny. "And thank goodness, so is . . . my mother's vase."

"I'm glad about the

vase," said Fagin. "Nice catch. But I'm even more glad that you're in one piece."

"Thank goodness you all were here," said Winston. "We might have spent our whole Christmas in the dark."

"Thank goodness you all were here," Jenny repeated.

"I can't imagine Christmas without you."

With Georgette in her lap, and Oliver purring on top

of the piano beside her, Jenny led Fagin in Christmas carols. He sang, "Wreck the Halls with Dogs of Folly," while the dogs howled and Oliver meowed along.

DISNEY'S
THE LITTLE MERMAID

ARIEL'S CHRISTMAS UNDER THE SEA

Ever since she had first gone to the water's surface, Ariel could do little but dream of life on land. Night after night, despite her father King Triton's command, Ariel swam to the surface to gaze at the beautiful palace, shining in the clear moonlight. She

was followed by her friend Flounder, and trailed by

Sebastian the crab, who had been instructed by Triton

to look after his daughter.

One winter evening she turned to her friend, her

eyes bright. "Look, Flounder! What are all those

beautiful lights lining the hill? They glow like stars, but they're so close to Earth!"

Flounder's large eyes grew even bigger as he gazed landward.

"They seem to be coming from the castle."

Each evening at sunset, Ariel and Flounder returned to their favorite cove to watch the lights go on. Each night, the castle grew brighter. Then not only the castle, but the castle grounds twinkled in the night, like the Milky Way.

One night as they watched, Scuttle the gull landed on their rock. "I see you're watching the Fooltide," he said.

Ariel was delighted to see Scuttle. He was an expert on human life, or at least he said he was.

"Fooltide?"

"When the foolish humans greet each other with glad

tidings. It's also known as 'The Hollydays', because they deck the halls with holly."

"But what are those twinkling lights?" asked Ariel.

"People light candles to welcome the season. Too

bad you can't take a peek inside the castle windows!"

Scuttle went on to describe the enormous decorated tree that stood in the great hall of the castle, the long tables piled high with roasts and puddings. He told how, as tokens of their love, humans bestowed gifts on one another, scattering bright wrappings everywhere

and shouting, "Merry Kris-Mess."

"Ah, yes," said Scuttle, "the Hollydays are something to behold."

Ariel listened in rapture. How she would love to be included in the festivities. She dreamed of taking part in decorating, singing, dancing, eating, and exchanging of gifts. But none of this could

happen unless she became a human. Followed by Flounder, Ariel swam back sadly to her father's kingdom.

"I don't want to see the castle's lights anymore," she told Flounder. "I can never share the humans' Hollydays."

Flounder hated to see Ariel unhappy. He rattled his

brain, and finally ventured, "We *could* make our own celebration."

Ariel brightened. "Why not? We could decorate the great hall. And I can look for gifts for my sisters. For Daddy, too. When he finds out about the Hollydays,

maybe he'll realize that humans are not such barbarians."

The days that followed were exhausting. Ariel,

Flounder, and Sebastian searched far and wide for the most beautiful seashells, sea stars, and water plants they could find. After decking the great hall, Ariel and her friends shaped a large tree from deep green strands of seaweed, and hung its limbs with colored glass circles made from bottles.

"And now for candles." Ariel searched her grotto, where she kept souvenirs gleaned from shipwrecks. The candlesticks were there, but the candles had all floated to the surface.

Ariel pleaded with Scuttle, "Please, can you find us some candles? They're the very best part."

"No problem," he said. "I think I can *borrow* a few."

Along the shore near the mouth of the river, Ariel found some magnificent moonstones, pebbles washed from the hills by a river and polished to brilliance by the waves of the sea. "Aha!" She gathered up the stones. They would make the perfect gift for her family, a gift that would help them understand how she felt.

Meanwhile, each day Flounder swam up and down the shore, seeking a gift for Ariel, one that would remind her of the land she loved.

One day he saw a young man pacing the beach, looking sad and lonely. As this man turned, a button fell from his shirt, a crystal button that sparkled in the sand.

When the tides came in, Flounder retrieved the button. He wrapped it in seaweed and tied it with a narrow ribbon.

The Hollyday Eve came at last. Ariel's heart strummed with excitement as she wrapped the gifts for her family in the petals of an anemone.

After she and Flounder had fixed Scuttle's candles onto the tree, Ariel blew through a large shell horn to summon her father, King Triton, and her sisters. "I have a surprise for you," she sang.

Ariel's family stared at the festive hall and the colorful tree. "What under the sea is this?" her sisters exclaimed.

"You mean, 'what on earth,'" bubbled Ariel. "This is Kris-Mess," she said proudly, "the way humans celebrate."

"It *is* splendid," they agreed, even King Triton.

"But just wait!" said Ariel. "Here's the best part."

She struck a flint to the candles. Nothing happened, for, of course, candles cannot burn underwater. She struck and struck again, her eyes filling with tears (although tears cannot flow underwater).

"It's all ruined," she wailed. "We've worked so hard. And now my Kris-Mess is a fizzle."

"Not so, my dear daughter," said Triton. "Though you cannot make candles burn as they do on land, you put your heart into this surprise. That's what makes it so special."

He took his
trident and aimed it
at the tree. The
candles glowed
with a magical
light. "There. Is
that better?"

From then on,
the evening was
filled with a magical spirit. Triton ordered up a grand
feast, accompanied by musicians. When Ariel presented

her gifts with "Happy Hollydays!" her family was overwhelmed. Her sisters held out the gleaming moonstones. "Where did you find these lovely gems?" Ariel explained how they were fashioned by both

earth and sea—working together as one. She looked up at her father, who merely smiled and nodded. He had understood the message of the moonstones.

Toward the end of the celebration, Flounder drew

Ariel aside. "I have something for you. Merry Kris-Mess!" He told her how he had found the gift.

"Flounder! How very precious!" Ariel took the crystal, laced the ribbon through the button, and hung it around her neck. The crystal rested near her heart.

When she held the bauble up to look at it, the crystal sparkled like starlight, like the lights that twinkled from the palace on the hill. As Ariel gazed at the light, she felt her heart glow with hope. And suddenly she knew the meaning of the candles in the night.

Disney's THE ARISTOCATS

AN ARISTOCAT-IC CHRISTMAS

A heavy snowfall had blanketed Paris. In the morning sun the city's walls and towers sparkled like icing on a cake.

Duchess sat on the windowsill, gazing at the magical scene. "Look, O'Malley. We're going to have a white Christmas!"

O'Malley, who was dozing in a velvet chair, sat up, turned toward Duchess, then said, "Well, how about that, Princess!"

"Snow makes Christmas even more special," said Duchess.

"Sure is pretty. But," said O'Malley, "winter can get pretty cold, and food is in short supply." The very thought brought his spirits down.

O'Malley was happy living in Madame Bonfamille's luxurious mansion, with his beloved Duchess and her three talented kittens: Berlioz, Toulouse, and Marie. Madame pampered them with fine foods and soft cushions and rides in her elegant coach. But sometimes O'Malley missed his old friends from the alleys, and often felt guilty that he was warm and well-fed while others still scavenged trash cans for scraps of food.

"Today Madame is decorating for the holiday," said Duchess. "Wait till you see what's coming. You'll get excited, too."

O'Malley thought over how he could see his friends during the holidays.

Preparations were indeed exciting, especially for the kittens, who stayed in the midst of all the bustle, crackling the tissue paper, unrolling spools of ribbon, swinging from the branches of the immense Christmas tree.

Madame smiled patiently at their antics. "Have your fun now, my little dears. When all is ready, you must behave yourselves."

By Christmas Eve, the whole house glittered with Christmas cheer. In the drawing room near the grand piano, a Christmas tree nearly touched the arched ceiling. It bore every kind of shiny ornament: golden birds and butterflies, moons and stars, glass globes and flowers. Golden tinsel swathed the branches, and at the tip of each, a candle flickered.

"See?" said Duchess to O'Malley. "Isn't Christmas magnificent?"

"Sure, Duchess," he

said. "But . . ."

"Isn't Christmas fun? said Duchess. "Come see Madame wrapping her gifts. You've never seen such packages!"

Duchess led him to the study, where Madame was tying a yellow bow on her final package, one of an enormous pile.

"There," said Madame. "We're ready for Christmas!"

Then Duchess led O'Malley down the hallway.

"And that's not all," said Duchess. "I'll show you the best part."

As they entered the kitchen, a host of heavenly smells prickled O'Malley's nose. Spicy puddings, apple tarts, roast goose.

"Ummm," said O'Malley. "This *could* be the best part."

"What do you mean, *could be*?" asked Duchess.

O'Malley said nothing, but grinned for the first time all day.

The next day brought a flurry of unwrapping, as

guests bearing gifts poured in and out of the mansion. Madame made a great pile of the discarded wrappings and let Berlioz, Toulouse, and Marie dance through them until the kittens were worn out.

When all the guests left, Madame brought out three more packages that she had set aside. These brightly colored bundles were gifts for the kittens. Toulouse

got a new set of paints, Berlioz some new sheet music, and Marie received a silver bell necklace that tinkled as she sang.

Duchess smiled as she watched the kittens. She called to O'Malley, "*Now* do you see what I mean about Christmas?"

But O'Malley had disappeared.

Madame sat at the end of the dining table, which was richly set with poinsettias and golden candelabra. To her right sat Duchess and the three kittens. The place on her left, set for O'Malley, was empty.

"Where can O'Malley be?" Duchess pouted to herself. "It's not right to keep Madame waiting."

Just then they heard a great clatter at the front door. In strutted O'Malley, followed by his old friend Scat Cat and his band.

The alley cats meowed.

"Welcome!" said Madame. "And Merry Christmas to you all!"

The band

members sat down at the table. They were followed by a crowd of the stray cats who had saved Duchess and the kittens from being sent to Timbuktu.

Madame rang for the butler. "You may now bring in the roast goose." She smiled and added, "But first my guests must play for their supper."

Scat Cat and his friends started with "Jingle Bells."

It was the jumping-est, jivey-est jingling that has ever jangled a Christmas day.

Amidst all the merriment, O'Malley whispered to himself, "Now, this is Christmas!"

And from the look of things, nobody disagreed.

Walt Disney's

Bambi

THE WONDERFUL WINTER TREE

Bambi awoke one morning to find a fluffy white blanket covering the whole world.

"This is snow," said his mother. "It means winter is upon us."

"Snow?" said Bambi. He walked in a circle and felt the cold snow crunch under his hooves as he made tracks round and round. "I like snow."

"Snow is pretty to look at, but winter can be hard," said his mother. "Especially when we animals can't find food."

Just then Thumper called to Bambi from a frozen pond. "Hiya, Bambi! Why don'tcha come sliding? Look, the water's stiff!" Bambi nuzzled his mother

good-bye and pranced off
to join his friend.

Flower came over to
see what was going on.
"You wanna come skat-
ing?" Bambi asked. "The
water's stiff."

"No, thanks," said the
skunk. "I'm ready to
settle down for a long
winter nap."

He called to the squirrel, who stood in the hollow of his oak tree. "The pond is stiff. Come sliding."

"Thanks, but I'm storing nuts for the long winter."

The chipmunk was in his nest, and the bear was asleep in his cave. Bambi went to the pond alone, where he found Thumper whooping it up with his rabbit friends.

For Bambi, the skating was not as much fun nor as easy as it looked. After dozens of flops on the ice, he was both bruised and hungry. So, Bambi set off to find his mother.

"Mother, I'm hungry," he said.

He looked for a patch of
grass, but all was covered over.

"Today we'll have to search
for our dinner," she said.

Following his mother,
Bambi poked through the snow
until he thought his nose would
freeze. They finally uncovered a mound of greens.
Bambi's mother watched over him as he ate.

Then they curled up in the thicket for a long nap,
their bodies huddled against the chilly air. Before

falling asleep Bambi turned to his mother. "Winter sure is long, isn't it?"

Day after day the animals spent most of their time in search of food. Bambi and his mother, often followed by Thumper, scoured the forest, sometimes with little luck. "Mother," asked Bambi, "is this why the birds fly south, and why our other friends sleep through the winter?"

His mother nodded yes, and gently nuzzled him.

The sun had set. It was almost time for sleep, but Bambi had found little to eat except some bitter bark. Then, at the edge of the valley he and his mother came upon a wondrous sight—a tall, snow-covered pine tree, draped top to bottom with strings of berries and

popcorn. From each branch hung a ripe green apple.

"Mother!" cried Bambi. "Look!"

Slowly, cautiously,

his mother drew closer.

"It seems too good to be

true," she whispered.

"What is it, Mother?"

asked Bambi.

"The most beautiful

tree I've ever seen," she

said. "He must have known that this was your first Christmas, Bambi."

"Who, Mother? Who?" Bambi was so hungry, he could almost taste those juicy apples.

"Santa Claus," explained Thumper.

"Santa Claus?" said Bambi. "Who's that? And what's a Christmas?"

Thumper and Bambi's mother explained that Santa was a jolly, magical elf who visited just around the time of the first snowfall each year. They told Bambi all about how he delivered presents and holiday cheer, and about his reindeer and sleigh.

"It was Santa who hung those berries and apples," said Thumper. "And put that star on the top."

After calling the good news to other animals, Bambi and his mother, along with Thumper, gathered to share the feast.

As they ate, they noticed a bright star in the heavens, a star like the one atop the pine tree. And as it shone, a hush settled over the valley, the sound of silence, of peace on earth.

When he gazed at the star, Bambi felt warm inside, and his heart swelled with the hope that spring would soon arrive.

WALT DISNEY'S

DUMBO

THE BEST CHRISTMAS

"Christmas is just around the corner," Timothy Q. Mouse told Dumbo.

Because of heavy snows, the Ringmaster had canceled the circus until after the holidays.

The young elephant, who hadn't yet been around for a full year, gave Timothy a puzzled look.

"Aw, c'mon, you know about Christmas, don'tcha?" said Timothy.

Dumbo shook his head.

"Bells jingling, trees twinkling, tissue paper crackle-crinkling?"

"Gifts and feasts with fancy eats," said the crows. "Deck the halls and wrap the dolls."

"You will love Christmas?" said Timothy.

"Everyone *loves* Christmas," said the crows. "At least most people do."

They huddled with Timothy, talking in low voices. Then Timothy said to Dumbo, "Come with us. We'll show you Christmas."

With the crows leading and Timothy on his back,

Dumbo flew through the crisp winter air.

The friends flew until they saw the New York City

skyline silhouetted against a blazing sunset. The crows

swooped down and landed on the roof of a tall building.

Below them the street sparkled with a million white

lights. An enormous tree, ablaze in color, overlooked an ice rink filled with skaters. Bumper-to-bumper cars honked at one another, and people carrying bright packages moved faster than the skaters.

"Now *this* is Christmas," said Timothy.

Dumbo's eyes grew wide as he looked down upon all the holiday lights and decorations.

"We can show you other kinds of Christmases," said the crows. "Then you can decide what kind you like best."

The crows flew across the river, where they led

Dumbo to the window of a cozy home. The room was decorated with a twinkly lighted tree and sparkling garlands. A woman looked on as her children hung their stockings by the fire and sang "Jingle Bells."

Timothy explained about Santa Claus, how he flew through the air bringing gifts to children.

Dumbo's heart filled with gladness. If this happy family scene was Christmas, he wanted to be a part of it.

"You'd better see more Christmases before you decide," said the crows.

On their next stop they perched on the fire escape of an old, run-down building. Looking in, they saw a large

family huddled around a stove, sharing soup out of a kettle. There was no tree, and not a single package.

Dumbo didn't understand why everyone couldn't have a jingly, twinkly, crackle-crinkly Christmas.

"They have no money," Timothy explained. He could tell that seeing this family had deeply affected Dumbo.

But Dumbo had an idea. He swooped off into the
night, Timothy clinging to his back. Dumbo returned to
their first stop, at the tall building and
the ice rink. He circled the huge
Christmas tree, doing loop-
the-loops and spins until he
caught the attention of the
crowd below.

Then he went into his
most dazzling circus act,
the one that had made

him famous. The shoppers and skaters stopped in their tracks, oohing and ahhing. When Dumbo was finished they cheered for more.

Then an amazing thing happened. People opened up their overloaded bags and donated packages.

After his encore flight, Dumbo collected a Santa-sized sack of presents.

Then Dumbo and his friends flew through the windows of all the families they could find without Christmases, giving them a jingly, twinkly, crackle-crinkly, Merry Christmas.

It was late when they returned to the circus, and snow was falling.

"Ahh," said Timothy. "That is the feeling of Christmas!"

And that night Dumbo fell asleep dreaming of sugarplums and fairies and Christmas trees all aglow.

DISNEY'S

Beauty and the BEAST

THE ENCHANTED CHRISTMAS

The Beast stormed up and down the great hall of his dark and gloomy castle. "I hate Christmas," he roared to Forte, the pipe organ. "That was the day my life ended," he added, remembering how his selfishness had caused him to be turned into a beast on Christmas Day.

In the days before the evil curse,

Forte had been court composer. Of all the enchanted objects, he was the only one who did not want to be human again. As long as the Beast remained unhappy, Forte could play his gloomy music.

Not knowing how the Beast felt about the holidays, beautiful Belle, who was a guest in the palace, decided to surprise him with a Christmas celebration, a

celebration so merry it would lift him from his misery.

Belle had Mrs. Potts plan a feast, and she asked the other servants to gather ribbons and tinsel. But when Belle went to the attic to find ornaments, Angelique, the Christmas tree angel, protested, "Here? Christmas?

I refuse to hope for it anymore. I will not be disappointed again." She knew the Beast would never allow a Christmas celebration.

Despite Angelique's warning, Belle continued to decorate. When all the rooms were twinkling, she went to fetch a yule log.

The Beast saw her and snatched it from her. "There will be no Christmas!" he thundered.

Belle refused to give up hope. "Well, I'm not giving up! Hmph!" she said. But Forte had other ideas—evil ones.

When Belle could not find a Christmas tree near the castle,

Forte suggested she search in the Black Forest.

"But I promised the Beast I would never leave the grounds," said Belle. "I gave my word."

"Never mind that," lied Forte. "The tree was always his favorite part of Christmas."

That was all Belle needed to hear. She and Chip, the

teacup, set out for the forest, followed reluctantly by Fife, the flute, who was part of Forte's wicked plan.

Gazing into his enchanted mirror, the Beast saw Belle riding away in a sleigh. "I didn't think she'd leave me," he said. The Beast felt very sad, for he loved Belle dearly.

Forte was pleased to see his plan was working—

the Beast was furious with Belle.

"I'll bring her back!" howled the Beast. He stormed through the castle, destroying all the Christmas decorations.

Meanwhile in the forest, Fife's piping frightened Philippe. The horse reared, hurtling the sleigh and Chip into the river. When Belle jumped in to save Chip, she was swept under the ice!

Just then the Beast appeared. He plunged

into the icy water to rescue Belle.

But after carrying her back to the castle, he locked her in the dungeon.

"You broke your word," he growled.

Lonely and defeated, the Beast returned to his bedroom. There he found a Christmas gift from Belle, a book she had written just for him. It began:

Once upon a time there was an enchanted castle. This castle's master seemed as cold as winter. But deep inside his heart . . .

The Beast realized that Belle had seen through his misery to the goodness he kept hidden inside!

He called his servants and spoke to them. Then he hurried to the dungeon. "Belle, can you forgive me?"

"Of course," Belle smiled.

When Forte realized that the Beast and Belle were friends again,

the jealous organ blasted his music throughout the castle, causing walls to quake and stones to tumble. He would destroy the place!

"Forte!" the Beast thundered. He ran to stop the  music. But it was too late. By his own forceful playing, Forte had torn himself away from the wall, tumbled over, and smashed into a thousand pieces.

When the dust cleared, the staff was bewildered.

Finally the Beast spoke. "What are we standing

around for? Let's give Belle the Christmas she's

always wanted."

The Beast opened the doors to a room decorated with an enormous Christmas tree. He escorted Belle into the room, where they were greeted by the enchanted objects.

The Beast and Belle began a celebration that they would never forget, especially the Beast. For on that Christmas Day, Belle gave him the gift of hope—the hope that someday the curse upon him would be lifted and life in the castle would begin again.

Flik's Christmas Invention

It was almost Christmas, and the ant colony was busier than ever. Not only did they have to store food for the long winter, but on their days off they tried

to finish their holiday gathering, wrap all the gifts, and prepare foods for the Yuletide feast.

"We'll never get it all done!" Princess Dot complained to Flik.

"We all work too hard

at Christmas," said Flik, "and rush too much. There must be a way to make it easier."

Princess Dot smiled. She always brought her problems to Flik, knowing that he would take them to heart. And now that he had become the colony's Official Inventor, she felt sure that he  would come up with one of his whiz-bang solutions.

Sure enough, on Christmas Eve, Flik came to her,

grinning cheek to cheek. "I've done it!" he cried. "Look here!"

He towed behind him a large machine made of hooks and rollers and wheels and spools sticking out every which way.

The contraption made no sense to Dot, but she managed to say, "How nice."

At that moment Queen Atta appeared. She looked aghast at the machine. "And *now* what . . . ?"

"It's my new work-saving device," said Flik proudly.

"Why should we save work?" asked Atta. "We already have more than enough to go around."

"But this machine will take the trouble and effort out of Christmas," said Flik.

"I don't know, Flik . . ." said Atta. "It seems that that's what Christmas means, making an extra effort to please those we love. Show me an easy Christmas, and I'll show you someone who doesn't care." With that she left the room.

Flik could not conceal his disappointment. Talk about effort. He'd spent *days* working on his Christmas machine.

"Never mind," said Dot. "When she sees this thingamajig in action, Atta will change her tune."

"You believe in me, don't you?" asked Flik. "That my work can make a difference in our world?"

"Let's get started," said Dot. "I have a pile of gifts to wrap."

Word about the wrapping machine spread quickly, and by suppertime the ants, laden with packages, were lined up to use the invention.

Flik took each box and placed it carefully on the

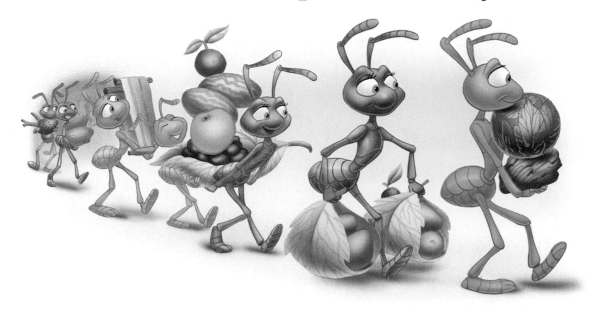

conveyor belt. When all were loaded, Flik called,
"Stand back now!"

He pulled the START lever. Twig levers moved, the
bark conveyor belt hummed. Leaf paper rattled, bright
petals unfurled, spools of grass whirled. The group
stared in awe. "Splendid.
Sensational.
Stupendous."

Flik's heart
raced as he
cranked the

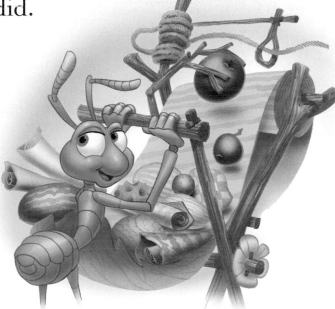

machine. In a few minutes' time everyone in the colony would be ready for Christmas. And all because of him.

Then the conveyor belt jammed. The packages piled up. The wrapping roller came down with a thud. *Clunk, crackle, crash!*

"Help! Our gifts! There goes Christmas!" cried the ants.

Flik could say nothing but "I'm sorry!" as he slunk away.

Dot tried to comfort him. "You were only trying to help."

"Maybe Atta was right," said Flik. "I was trying to make Christmas too easy. Maybe we *do* need to show some effort for those we care about."

"It's not too late," said Dot. "I have an idea."

And in whispers they made a plan.

That evening a curtain was drawn across the great hall. From behind it came the sounds of great hustle-bustle. "What's going on in there?" said Atta.

"No peeking!" cried Dot.

On Christmas morning all was peaceful. Then came

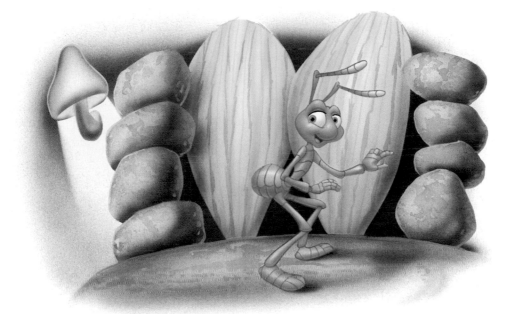

a loud knock at the door. Flik, wearing a mistletoe wreath, opened it wide.

"Merry Christmas!" In filed the colony's old friends, the circus bugs: Francis the ladybug, Rosie the spider, Dim the beetle, Heimlich, who was a beautiful butterfly, Slim the walking stick, Manny the mantis, and Gypsy the moth. Pill bugs Tuck and Roll brought up the rear.

"Welcome!" said Flik, pulling back the curtain. "Our feast is ready."

A beautifully decked table ran the length of the hall,

covered with every kind of treat, from honeycombs to cranberries. At the end of the room, an evergreen branch flickered brightly.

Atta swooshed into the room. "What a fantastic feast! How did you ever pull this together?"

"It wasn't easy," said Dot.

"It *was* work," Flik admitted. "But work is fun when

you're doing it for friends."

"Flik, my friend." Atta smiled. "I think you've helped us all understand more about the true meaning of Christmas."

Then ants and bugs feasted and sang and danced until the moon had risen and set.

Walt Disney's

Lady and the TRAMP

Lady's Christmas Surprise

The week before Christmas, Tramp and the puppies gathered beneath Jim and Darling's brightly decorated tree. "Do any of you kids know," Tramp asked, "what your mother'd like for Christmas?"

The puppies shook their heads.

"How about a new ball?" said Scamp. "Hers is all worn out."

"That's the way she likes it," said Tramp. "In fact, she traded hers for mine."

The second puppy, Annette, said, "A steak from Tony's Restaurant?"

Tramp shook his head. "Lady says she's on a diet."

"We need to give her something special," said the

third, Colette, "to show how much we love her."

"A jeweled collar?" said the fourth, Scooter.

"I can't afford one," said Tramp, "and now that I'm a family man, I've lost my taste for theft."

"Why don't you ask her what she'd like?" said Scamp.

"We want to surprise her," said Tramp. "That's the fun of Christmas."

So Lady's family trotted into town to get some gift ideas.

The village bustled with shoppers, their carriage wheels carving dark ruts in the snowbanked roadway. At the chemist's shop, one of the coaches pulled to a

stop, spattering mud on Tramp and the puppies. Out stepped an elegant bejeweled woman. When she saw the muddy dogs she shrieked, "Get away, you filthy mutts!" She swung her walking stick at them, clapping Tramp across the nose. Then she sashayed across the sidewalk and disappeared from sight.

Tramp rubbed his nose. "Some Christmas spirit she has!"

The dogs

rambled up and down the avenue, looking in all the shop windows. There was no shortage of gift ideas: sweaters, cushions, brush and comb sets. But Tramp

knew he couldn't get any of these things for Lady. Finally, he said to the puppies, "We'd better head for the alleys and dig something from the trash."

Crossing the road, Tramp noticed something

sparkling in the snowdrift. It was much brighter than an icicle. He turned it over with his paw. "Holy hambones!" It was a necklace, a gold and diamond necklace! Tramp took it into his mouth.

"What a bunch of rocks!" said Scamp.

"What a beautiful stroke of luck!" said Annette.

"Just the right size for Mother!" said Colette.

Scamp asked, "Wasn't that mean woman wearing a necklace like that?"

"Serves her right!" said Scamp.

Tramp smiled, and the necklace dropped onto the

snow. It sparkled in the sunlight. It *would* look beautiful on Lady.

"But . . ." His face darkened. "No. That wouldn't be right. Sorry, kids, we gotta return the necklace."

He picked up the bauble and scampered back to the sidewalk where they had seen the woman. Her carriage was gone.

"Hooray," cheered Scamp. "We tried, didn't we?"

"Not hard enough," said Tramp. With the puppies following, he bounded down the block, to a building where a white round lamp read: POLICE.

Inside, Tramp trotted up to the desk and dropped the necklace in front of the policeman in charge.

"What's this?" said the officer.

Tramp panted and wagged his tail.

"You found it?"

Tramp nodded.

"Good dog!"

The policeman

took the necklace and

began filling out his

report, noting on it

Tramp's name and address, which were engraved on his

collar tag.

At that moment the mean woman rushed into the station. "I've been robbed!" She rattled on in such a twitter she didn't notice the dogs, who were sitting quietly behind the policeman's desk. "The necklace is a family heirloom.

I'll give a handsome reward for its return."

The policeman winked at the dogs and said,
"How much?"

After the woman had left with her necklace, the
policeman tucked an envelope under Tramp's collar.
Inside was the cash reward and a note that said:

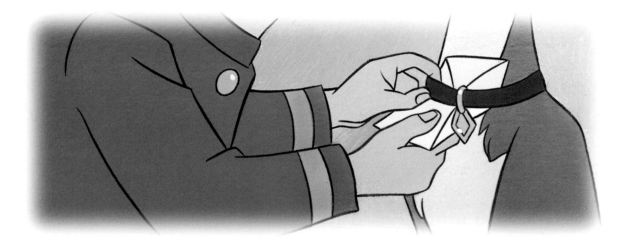

To whom it may concern: Your dogs are to be commended for their honesty in turning over to the police a valuable piece of lost merchandise. Signed, Captain Quirk

Tramp, with the puppies in tow, raced to the harness maker. Standing with front paws on the counter, he looked at an assortment of beautiful jeweled collars. He found one with green stones and picked it up with his mouth.

"Hold on, there!" cried the shopkeeper.

One of the puppies took the envelope from Tramp's collar and dropped it at the man's feet. The man read the note. "Good dogs!" He took the cash, and returned change to the envelope. "And smart, too!"

On Christmas morning Lady tore open the gift. "You shouldn't have!" Her eyes sparkled like the green stones.

When Darling fastened the collar around Lady's neck, she pranced around the room like a show dog.

Suddenly she stopped. "Tramp, you didn't . . . you wouldn't . . .?" Her bright eyes grew worried.

Tramp brought Jim Dear the envelope. He read, *"To whom it may concern. . . ."*

When he finished the note, Jim said, "I'm proud of you, Tramp."

"I love my collar," said Lady. She nuzzled Tramp and the puppies. "But even more, I love my family—my honest family."

"Merry Christmas," said Darling. And as a special treat, she set six bowls of kidney pudding on the hearth.

Walt Disney's MICKEY MOUSE

Mickey's Christmas Carol

Scrooge hurried past the carolers, who called to him, "Give a penny for the poor, Gov'ner?"

"Bah!" Scrooge replied.

He climbed the steps to his office, and with his cane knocked snow from the sign SCROOGE & MARLEY, still not replaced. Jacob Marley, his partner, had died seven years ago that very evening. He and Scrooge had built a good business robbing widows and swindling the poor.

Inside the office, Scrooge's clerk, Bob Cratchit, shivered as he copied letters. Surely Scrooge wouldn't miss a little coal.

As he lifted the scuttle, Scrooge burst into the room. "What are you doing with that piece of coal?"

"I was—ha, ha—just trying to thaw out the ink," replied Bob.

"Bah! You used a piece last week!"

As Scrooge sat at his desk, weighing his gold coins, the door burst open. "Merry Christmas!"

Scrooge's nephew Fred came in, holding a wreath.

"Christmas?" snorted Scrooge. "Humbug."

"I don't care. Merry Christmas!" Fred handed his uncle the wreath. "I've come to invite you to dinner."

"Are you daft, man? You know I can't eat all that stuff!" Scrooge kicked his nephew out the door. "Here's your wreath back. Now out! Out!"

After Fred left, Scrooge turned to Cratchit. "And I

suppose you expect tomorrow off?"

"Why, yes, sir."

"Then make sure you come in early the day after!"

That night at Scrooge's home, he heard the sound of clanking chains. The ghost of his partner, Jacob Marley, appeared.

Scrooge was terrified.

"Ebenezer, remember when I was alive, I robbed the widows and swindled the poor?" wailed Marley. "As punishment, I'm forced to carry these heavy chains through eternity."

He shook the chains wildly. "And the same thing will happen to you.

"Tonight you will be visited by three spirits. Listen to 'em. Do what they say, or your chains'll be heavier than mine." With a clink and a clank of his chains, Marley disappeared.

Later, as Scrooge slept, a little man appeared in a top hat. "I am the ghost of Christmas Past," he said. "We're gonna visit your

past. Just hold on—woo!—not too tight, now!"

Remembering Marley's warning, Scrooge grabbed

and held on tight as the man flew out into the darkness. Soaring over rooftops, they landed by a cottage window. Looking in, Scrooge saw his

young love,

Isabelle, dancing

with a smiling

young man.

"That was you,"

said the spirit,

"before you

became a miserable miser consumed by greed."

The spirit whisked Scrooge to another scene,

Scrooge's office. Isabelle was crying. Scrooge

remembered that he had foreclosed on Isabelle's cottage

and had lost her forever.

He awoke in his bed.

Scrooge felt a heavy

hand on his shoulder. A

fierce voice boomed,

"I am the ghost of

Christmas Present."

Scrooge saw a giant

peering in through the

roof. The giant snatched him from the covers and

carried him into the night.

The next thing Scrooge knew they were at Cratchit's shabby house. Through the window he could see the family about to carve a small, scrawny goose. A boy on a crutch hobbled into the room. It was Bob's son, Tiny

Tim. "If these shadows remain unchanged, I see an empty chair where Tiny Tim once sat," said the spirit.

The scene shifted to a later time. Scrooge

landed in a graveyard, facing a hideous dark specter. "Are you the ghost of Christmas Future?" Scrooge asked. But the spirit just pointed.

Church bells tolled. The Cratchits sobbed over a gravesite. Scrooge realized that Tiny Tim was dead.

"Tell me these events can yet be changed!" Scrooge

pleaded.

The spirit pointed

to a deep pit.

"Whose lonely

grave is this?"

asked Scrooge.

"Why, yours,

Ebenezer," replied

the spirit.

The spirit slapped Scrooge on the back.

"Oh, nooo!" Scrooge tumbled into the pit. As he fell, he remembered all the people he had wronged. "I'll change! Let me out! Let me . . ."

Scrooge once more awoke in his bed. The sun shone bright; Christmas bells

were ringing. "It's Christmas morning!" he stammered. "I haven't missed it! The spirits have given me another chance!"

He threw on his hat and coat and dashed outside. "Merry Christmas!" called the people on the street.

"Merry Christmas to one and all!"

Scrooge cried as he pushed gold coins into the hands of the folks collecting money for the poor.

He hurried past his nephew's carriage. "Ah, nephew!" he called. "I'm looking forward to that wonderful meal of yours!"

Rat-a-tat-tat! Bob Cratchit heard a sharp knock at

his door. When he opened it, his face fell. Scrooge, looking very cross, stood with a big sack.

"I've brought another bundle for you," he said, holding a laundry bag.

"B-but, sir, it's Christmas Day," said Bob.

Scrooge threw the sack on the floor. Out fell dozens

of parcels tied with bright ribbons. He grinned as he watched the children's faces light with joy.

Then Scrooge offered the family the most wonderful gift of all. "Bob Cratchit," he said, "I'm giving you a raise, and making you my new partner!"

Mrs. Cratchit then discovered the Christmas turkey Scrooge bought for them.

"Merry Christmas, Bob!" Scrooge smiled.

The whole family danced with joy. The children would never go hungry. Tiny Tim could grow stronger.

Seeing their merry faces, Ebenezer Scrooge was

happy for the first time in many years. How good it feels, he thought, to be generous and kind.

"God bless us, every one," said Tiny Tim.

Pinocchio

PINOCCHIO'S PERFECT GIFT

It was almost Christmas, and Geppetto was frantically busy making toy soldiers and dolls. In fact, Santa himself had placed a big order because his elves were behind schedule. Each day, as Geppetto carved and glued and painted, he grew more rushed and weary.

Meanwhile, Pinocchio, with the help of Jiminy Cricket, was getting the house ready for his first Christmas as a real boy. He and Jiminy had put up a tree, strung garlands of holly from the rafters, and even baked a plum pudding.

"Jiminy, I want to find the perfect gift for Geppetto," said Pinocchio. "Will you help me?"

"Well, if you ask me . . ." Jiminy began.

But Pinocchio was too excited to listen. He was already out the door, and on his way to the shops.

Jiminy caught up with him at the cutlery shop.

"How about a new knife?" said Pinocchio. "I'll

take the black one." Pinocchio pulled out his coins.

The shopkeeper shook his head. "I'm sorry, son. The poorest of my wares costs ten times what you have."

Undaunted, Pinocchio dashed into another store.

They shopped for socks, for gloves, for caps to keep

Geppetto warm while he worked. A chest to keep his tools in. An armchair to relax in. But everything was too small, too big, or too expensive.

Now it was Christmas Eve, and the shopkeepers were locking their doors. It was time to return home.

"Jiminy," cried Pinocchio, "what am I going to do?"

"Well, you know, I did have this idea—" Jiminy replied with a sigh.

"Really?" said Pinocchio. "Why didn't you say so before?"

Jiminy sat Pinocchio at the kitchen table. "You want to give your father something he really needs?"

"I sure do," beamed Pinocchio. "More than anything, I do."

Jiminy handed Pinocchio a pen and paper. "Write what I tell you." He dictated:

Dear Geppetto: This will entitle you to an extra pair of hands, an extra pair of legs, and an extra-willing heart. Your loving son, Pinocchio

"But—but, Jiminy! It's just a scrap of paper," said Pinocchio. "What sort of gift is that?"

Jiminy took the note, put it in a box, and tied it with a red ribbon. "If you ask me, what the poor man really

needs is help! All the work he has can't be done alone. Now, let's get to the workshop."

When Geppetto opened Pinocchio's gift, he was overjoyed. "Well, now, I guess I *could* use a pair of hands."

Pinocchio scurried about the workshop, sweeping up shavings, tending the fire, boxing and wrapping toys. He finally finished at midnight, and just in time, for at the stroke of twelve there came a thump on the roof, then a clatter that shook the whole house. Santa had come to pick up the bundle of gifts that Geppetto had made.

At the window appeared the jolly old elf. "Phew," he said,

"that was a close one, Geppetto. I can't thank you enough for helping out."

"Never would have made it without the help of my son," said Geppetto.

Santa took out his notebook. "I'll have to remember that."

That night, as Pinocchio slept, the Blue Fairy appeared to him.

"Santa sent me," she said. "Because you've been so thoughtful, he wanted me to drop off a Christmas wish."

"If you ask me. . . ." piped up Jiminy, who was perched on the headboard.

"I have an idea," said Pinocchio. "I know exactly what I want. I want the perfect gift for Geppetto."

The fairy smiled, "Very well. That's what we'll do."

Geppetto awoke early that morning and went to light the yule log. There, hanging from the Christmas tree, he found—oh, no, it couldn't be!—the puppet Pinocchio.

"Pinocchio!" He fell back into his chair. "My dear Pinocchio!"

Pinocchio and Jiminy came running from the bedroom. "What is it, Father?"

"My gift! How did you ever make it?"

Pinocchio turned toward the tree and saw the doll, a perfect copy of the puppet he used to be.

"Puppet Pinocchio was my favorite toy," said Geppetto,

"because I wanted him to be my son. Now I have both."

A shadow crossed Pinocchio's face. "You mean, you've missed the doll? Have I been a disappointment?"

"You've been a perfect son in every way, Pinocchio. Except you don't dance too well."

Geppetto pulled the puppet from the tree and danced him wildly around the room.

Stopping for breath, he added, "Because I'm a toymaker, no one has ever thought to give me a toy of my own to play with. Only you, Pinocchio, understood how much I love toys!"

Under the tree were a number of gifts for

Pinocchio, brought by Santa, perhaps, or made by Geppetto. But the Blue Fairy had sent him the best gift of all: the smile on his father's face.

Winnie the Pooh

Pooh's Jingle Bells

"Mmm," said Winnie the Pooh. "I love Christmas Eve. Tomorrow my stocking will be full of new honeypots."

"Getting presents is fun," said Christopher Robin, "but do you know what makes Christmas an especially important time of year?"

Pooh scratched behind his ear. He didn't quite remember.

"Christmas means thinking of others, and helping those in need."

"I'll bet Santa needs a hand about now," said Pooh, "with all those presents to deliver! If we only had a sleigh . . ."

". . . we could help him," finished Christopher Robin. "Let's go look for one."

They met Piglet outside his door, sweeping snow and singing "Jingle Bells."

"We're going to the North Pole to help Santa deliver gifts," said Pooh. "Just as soon as we find a sleigh."

"Oh, what a lovely idea," said Piglet. "I'd like to come, too, but I have to clear my walk."

"We'll help you," said Christopher Robin. And they did.

Next, they went to visit Roo, to see if he had a sleigh. They found him in his front yard, playing with his jingle bells.

"Sleigh bells!" cried Piglet.

"That must mean you have a sleigh," said Pooh.

"Do you have one?" asked Christopher Robin. "We want to take

it to the North Pole to help Santa deliver gifts."

"Wow!" said Roo. "I don't have a sleigh, but Tigger does. Or, anyway, a big sled. He'll be here soon. Maybe you can help Mama and me bake Christmas cookies until he comes."

And they did.

"Nummy yummy!" Tigger burst through the door. "I smell cookies."

"Tigger, may we borrow your sled?" asked Piglet. "We need to help Santa deliver gifts."

"Hey, that's a wunnerful idea!" said Tigger through a mouthful of crumbs.

Everyone piled onto Tigger's sled, and they swooshed down the hill.

They scrunched to a stop in front of Rabbit's house, where he stood with Owl and Eeyore.

"Are we at the North Pole yet?" asked Roo.

"The North Pole?" scoffed Rabbit.

"Not even close," said Eeyore.

"But you're just in time to help decorate the big pine tree," said Rabbit.

And they did, with bright shiny globes, popcorn chains, and twinkle lights.

"Oh d-d-dear!" said Piglet. "It's getting late. Perhaps we should hurry if we want to help Santa."

"And you're going in *this*?" Owl eyed Tigger's sled. "Where are your reindeer?"

"Oh!" said Pooh. "We forgot that part."

"Don't look at *me*," said

Eeyore.

But they did.

Rabbit tied Eeyore to

the sled. "The perfect

one-horse open sleigh!"

Eeyore puffed and

pulled and Piglet jingled

Roo's bells as everyone sang: "Bells on bobtail ring."

The sun sank behind the hills. "I've been thinking,"

said Christopher Robin with a shiver. "If we go to the North Pole, we won't have time to give presents to each other."

"Oh, no!" said Pooh. "*Getting* may not be an important part of Christmas. But *giving* is."

"Keep singing that nice jingly tune," said Eeyore, "and I'll

shoosh us home in no time." And he did.

Together they laughed and sang and jingled their way around the Hundred-Acre Wood, delivering presents to all their friends.

"We're Santa's helpers, after all," sang Pooh.

THE HUNCHBACK OF NOTRE DAME

CHRISTMAS IN THE BELL TOWER

From the bell tower, Quasimodo watched the snow fall, blanketing the city in white. It was Christmas Eve. Through the windows of the houses below, he could see blazing hearths and happy families gathered around lighted trees. "Paris is so beautiful at Christmas-

time," he sighed. "But, here I am, surrounded by cold stone walls, and all alone."

"What do you mean, *alone*?" scowled Victor. The gargoyles sprang to life. "What do you think *we* are?"

"Just part of the scenery?" added Hugo.

Old Laverne shuffled toward him. "Face it, boys. We don't count for much. Quasi's pining for a visit from his girlfriend."

"Esmeralda's not my girlfriend," Quasi protested.

"She's just a girl," said Victor.

"And a friend," said Hugo.

"The gypsies are having a big feast tonight," said Quasi. "Esmeralda's probably roasting a goose. There's no reason to hope . . ."

". . . that she'd have time to think of you," said Victor, winking at Hugo.

After Quasi had saved Esmeralda's life, she had promised to visit him often. And she had kept her word, up to now.

"You *could* go visit her," said Hugo.

"No," said Quasi. "I'm in charge of the bells. First I must ring vespers, then the midnight bells."

"Never mind," said Victor. "Why don't we make our own celebration?"

"This place *could* use a little cheer," said Hugo.

Laverne gave a loud whistle. Seconds later a row of

pigeons lined the parapet. She whispered to them, and off they flew.

Within moments they returned, carrying fir branches, holly boughs, and strands of mistletoe in their beaks. "Now, get to work, Quasi," said Laverne.

As Quasi decked the walls, he felt his loneliness leave. He *was* a part of Christmas after all.

"How about some candles?" said Victor. "It's frightfully dim in here."

Quasi went down to the cathedral and borrowed from the large supply of altar candles. Soon the place

was aglow, and every bit as festive as the homes in the city below.

For supper, Quasi brought out his usual bread and cheese. It seemed such humble fare for the richly bedecked table. "I should have thought," he said, "to fix a better meal."

"A feast is not what you eat," said Laverne. "It's who you share it with."

"You're right," said Quasi. "And I'm lucky to be with the most steadfast friends around."

"You got that right!" said Hugo with a grin.

Just then they heard footsteps on the stairway—hurried footsteps. Who could it be? The cathedral porter looking for his candles? The police checking for fire in the tower? The angry ghost of Frollo bent on ruining Christmas Eve?

The door burst open. Quasi gasped, "Esmeralda!"

"Merry Christmas!" she cried. In her outstretched arms she held a big platter of roasted goose.

She was followed by Djali and the band of gypsies, the men strumming and piping carols, and the women carrying baskets of bread and fruit, and

fancy Yuletide pastries. The gypsies hoped to make

Quasimodo's holiday very special this year.

Esmeralda looked around the beautifully decorated

tower room. "You told him!" she said to the

gargoyles.

Quasi shook his head. "I didn't know you would come. But I must admit I wished."

"And your wish has come true!" said Esmeralda.

She set about arranging Quasi's table with the Yuletide feast. But when she turned to him, he was gone. "Quasimodo!"

Then she heard the vesper bells ringing in Christmas Eve. They sounded more joyous than they ever had before.

TARZAN®

Disney's

CHRISTMAS IN THE JUNGLE

Jane looked around the tree house with a melancholy face.

"Do you feel all right?" asked Tarzan. "You don't seem your cheerful self."

Jane forced a smile. She was fine. Why shouldn't she be? She, Tarzan, and her father, Professor Porter, loved their life in the jungle, surrounded by their ape family and the other animals.

They had added rooms to the tree house until it was now almost like a mansion. And Tarzan was the bravest, strongest, kindest man a woman could ever want. Then why did she feel so blue?

She glanced at the calendar. December 23. "No wonder!" she said. "Without the change of seasons, I completely forgot. It's almost Christmas."

"So it is," chuckled Porter, who had been napping in his rocker.

"I'm going to miss it," sighed Jane.

"Christmas?" said Tarzan. "If you need a Christmas, I'll be glad to get you one." He would go to the ends of the earth to make Jane happy.

"Let me explain, Tarzan," said Jane. "Back home in England, where Daddy and I come from, Christmas is a holiday."

"A holiday," repeated Tarzan with a puzzled look on his face.

"Yes," continued Jane. "It's a day of celebration, the most beautiful day of the year."

She went on to describe snowfall and sleigh bells, pine trees and packages, tinsel and tender roast goose.

"I don't think I could bring you a snowfall," said Tarzan.

Jane brightened. "But maybe we can do the rest. Well, sort of, anyway."

"I don't see why not," said Porter. "Christmas is more than snow and sleigh bells. It's a time to share with friends. And we have plenty of them." He looked out toward the jungle.

The sun was setting beyond a glassy pond where

elephants were bathing. Among the trees that lined the shore they could see the dark shapes of their ape family.

As evening shadows lengthened, the darkness was filled with sounds of jungle creatures: chirps, screeches, growls, and roars. Jane smiled and turned to Tarzan. "As Father said," she explained, "Christmas is a time of sharing. Our friends need a Christmas, too!" She told him her plan. The next day, assisted by their ape family, Jane and Tarzan went through the jungle, picking its fruits and nuts. Tarzan found a small tree in the forest, which, with Jane's help, he shaped into a Christmas tree. They decorated the tree with garlands of bright berries. When all was finished, Tarzan set a paper star on the top.

"There is still something missing," said Jane. "Our tree doesn't have any lights."

"There are a few candles left," said Porter.

"That's a wonderful idea, Daddy," said Jane. "And I have another idea."

On Christmas Eve she and Tarzan captured hundreds of fireflies in small jars, leaving holes in the jar lids for the insects to breathe. They hung a jar on each tree limb. The tree sparkled with light.

From the tree house they looked down on their outdoor tree, where the animals were gathered, gazing in wonder. There were turtles and crocodiles; birds, elephants, and hippos; rhinos and zebras. There were graceful antelopes and awkward wildebeests; and, of course, the families of apes and baboons.

Into their midst strode the mighty cats—the lions, the leopards, the cheetahs. A hush fell over the jungle as the animals moved back to allow the fierce, powerful beasts to approach the tree.

"Look!" cried Jane. "They're all together around the tree, like . . ."

"It can't be!" said Tarzan.

". . . like one big happy

family," said Jane.

The lions, leopards, and cheetahs sat on their haunches, staring at the tree, then curled up like pussycats beneath its branches.

At that moment, a solitary bright star appeared in the sky, shining directly above the paper star of the decorated jungle tree.

"I do like Christmas," said Tarzan. "It's . . . it's
like magic."

Porter looked down at the peaceful animals in
amazement. He lit his pipe and shook his head.
"Why can't Christmas last all year round?"

Disney's ROBIN HOOD

CHRISTMAS FOR EVERYONE

On Christmas Eve, Robin Hood and his Merry Men were gathered together for the holiday celebration.

Robin Hood and Little John had roasted a goose and chestnuts over the open fire. The savory aromas filled the chilly air, drawing the men to the table.

"A true feast!" said Friar Tuck.

"We did our best," said Little John and Robin Hood.

But after they sat down to eat, the men were

strangely silent.

"Something's missing," said Toby Turtle.

"What is it, Toby?" asked Robin Hood. "Aren't you

enjoying the feast?"

"The cooking tastes fine," said Toby. "It's just that . . ."

"Maybe we need some Christmas music." Allan-a-Dale picked up his lute.

"I know what's missing," said Robin Hood. "We took the day off to get ready for Christmas. . . ."

". . . which means we didn't rob the rich," said Little John.

"... which means we didn't give to the poor," said Tuck.

"And Christmas is the one big day for giving," said Robin. "No wonder we don't feel right."

"It's not too late," said Allan-a-Dale. "The sun has not yet set."

Toby Turtle chimed in. "We can take this feast and . . ."

"Oh, no! Not the roasted goose." Tuck

was so looking forward to the meal.

"I have a better idea," said Robin. He rubbed his whiskers. "Let's see. Whose yule gifts shall we lift?"

Little John added, "Who deserves a feast the least?"

And Tuck chimed in with a grin, "Who'd take money from a church mouse to keep in his warehouse?"

The Merry Men answered in chorus: "The Sheriff of Nottingham!" And so they set off on their sleigh.

The Merry Men peeked through the sheriff's frosted windows. A yule log blazed on the hearth, his tree twinkled with candles, and the mantel was piled with

gifts. Steam rose from the large

dining table as the sheriff cut into his plum pudding.

"I'll go to the front door and distract him," said

Robin, "while you men sneak his Christmas out

through the kitchen."

Robin quickly disguised himself as a blind beggar and rapped on the sheriff's door. When the sheriff opened it, Robin said, "Alms for a poor blind man?"

"Fie!" The sheriff swung the door shut, but the blind man's cane held it open.

"Can you spare no alms on Christmas Eve?"

"Haven't I seen that outfit before?" said the sheriff.

"Hat and cloak and glasses . . ." He swelled with anger, and lunged forward to grab the beggar. "You don't fool me, Robin Hood!"

Robin loosed himself from the sheriff's grip and took flight. "I'll get you this time," the sheriff thundered, and ran off after him.

But his lumbering bulk was no match for Robin's speed. Robin

leaped into a tree and left the sheriff running circles in the forest.

Meanwhile, the Merry Men loaded their sleigh with brightly wrapped gifts, roast goose, and pudding, and even the magnificent Christmas tree.

Robin soon caught up with the sleigh. "There's no time

to waste. He's hopping mad."

Just then, Maid Marian and Lady Kluck, her lady-in-waiting, passed by in Maid Marian's carriage. She signaled the driver to stop. "Why, Robin Hood, what a

merry surprise!"

Robin bowed low to the ladies.

Maid Marian said, "I've been out delivering baskets to the poor."

"But there are so many in need this year," said Lady Kluck, "we have quite run out."

"It just so happens," said Robin, "I was doing the same. Let me share with you."

And before one could say "Nottingham," Robin and

the sheriff's Christmas trimmings were safely tucked

into the carriage. "See you back in Sherwood Forest,"

Robin called to his men.
"And remember to save
me a drumstick."

After the food and
gifts were distributed,
Robin and Maid
Marian left the
sheriff's Christmas tree

in the town square for all to enjoy.

Then they headed for Sherwood Forest to join the Merry Men, who had this night a Christmas that was truly merry.

Walt Disney's

Snow White
and the Seven Dwarfs

A CHRISTMAS TO REMEMBER

For many months, Snow White had lived quietly with the Seven Dwarfs, sharing their cozy cottage in the woods. When the dwarfs found out she was a princess, fleeing from her stepmother, the Queen, they had done everything they could to keep her safe and happy.

The girl loved the dwarfs — Doc, Grumpy, Happy, Sleepy, Sneezy, Bashful, and Dopey — as if they were her own family.

She cleaned, washed, and ironed for them, and each evening when they came home from the mines, she had a hot meal waiting.

One December morning, while Snow White was out feeding the forest birds, Doc sat down with the other six dwarfs. "Christmas is coming," he said. "What say we

give Snow White a gifty nift—er—a nifty gift!"

"We need to show our appreciation," said Happy, "for all she's done for us."

"Aw, why not! She deserves something, I guess," said Grumpy. Sleepy said, "She could use a new quilt for her bed."

"How about a lace handkerchief?"

suggested Sneezy.

"I have an idea,"
said Bashful, blushing.
"Why not give her
something from our
mines? Something
for her to remember
us by?"

"Remember us? She's
not going anywhere," said Grumpy, "is she?"

"Let's hope not," yawned Sleepy.

"If we work extra hard," said Doc, "we could find the perfect pimond—er—diamond. And we've already dug enough gold."

"We could make her a crown," said Happy. "A crown like a princess would wear."

"Snow White *is* a princess," Bashful reminded them, "in every way."

The next day the dwarfs busied themselves at the mine. In the cottage, Snow White got ready for Christmas, too. First, she made a tray of

special cookies, cutting them in shapes of bells and stars and Christmas trees.

While the cookies baked, she went into the forest
and cut down a dwarf-sized pine tree. She pulled it

home on a small sled,
gathering red berries
and boughs of holly on
her way.

When she returned,
the cottage smelled of
warm cinnamon and
sugar. The smell was so
delicious it made

Snow White quite hungry. But instead of nibbling on the cookies, she laced them on ribbons and hung each on the little pine tree. She draped strings of berries on the branches, singing carols all the while.

By the time she had finished decking the walls with holly and the beams with mistletoe, Snow White was tired and sat down by the fire to nap.

There came a knock, but Snow White had been warned by the dwarfs not to open her door to strangers. Through the window she saw an old hag returning to the forest, a basket of fruit on her arm.

I should have welcomed the poor woman, thought
Snow White, but she had to keep her promise to the
dwarfs. Little did she know that the visitor was the
wicked queen in disguise.

When the dwarfs came home and saw the tree, they danced and shouted with delight. "Merry Christmas!"

"What a treasure you are!" said Happy.

"Speaking of treasure," said Doc, "we have a little surprise for you." From his cloak he brought a small package wrapped in brown paper and placed it under the tree.

"No squeaking—er—peeking," he said. "You must wait until Christmas Eve."

On Christmas Eve, Snow White cooked a fine feast of roast fowl and a nut-filled plum pudding. During the evening her eyes strayed often to the lighted tree and to the package beneath it.

While living with her stepmother, she had not received a single gift.

When the last slice of pudding was gone and the dwarfs had washed the dishes, Doc at last handed Snow White the small bundle.

When she opened it,

Snow White gasped with delight. "Why, this is lovely! But how did you ever . . . ?"

"We made it," said Happy, proudly. "You're crying!" said Doc. "Didn't we do it right?" Snow White went to the mirror and put on the crown.

She felt like a princess once again.
"Oh, thank you," she said.
"This is wonderful—and
it is even more precious
because you put your
hearts into it."

"Shucks, 'twasn't
much," said Bashful.

Snow White wore
the splendid crown all
through the Christmas

holiday. Then she wrapped it carefully and tucked it away in a drawer, to save for the day when she might once again become a princess.

Andy's Christmas Puppy

On Christmas morning, the toys waited anxiously for the Green Army Men's report. The men had been sent on a recon mission to find out: (1) what Andy had gotten for Christmas and (2) if he had received any toy that he would love more than them.

The army men had no sooner set up their operation

when they heard the sound of barking. "Wow!" cried Andy. "A puppy!"

"We're dead!" said cowboy Woody to his friends. "Do you all know about puppies?"

Buzz Lightyear, the space ranger, looked blank. "Never heard of them."

"Puppies are some super-toy that's almost human,"

said Woody. "I mean, they wiggle and run and bark, and they don't need batteries. Kids are crazy about them."

"Whoa!" said Buzz.

"Not only that, they eat," said Woody. "I mean eat and swallow. But worse that that, they chew."

"Like Sid's dog?" asked Rex. The timid dinosaur trembled.

Cruel Sid, who used to live next door to Andy before they moved, often let his dog chew toys.

"Now, fellas," said Bo Peep. "You know Andy wouldn't let anything hurt you. He takes good care of his toys."

The group stood in shocked silence.

Just then Andy burst into the bedroom, carrying the

dreaded puppy in his arms. He sat the puppy on his bed, but it immediately bounded off, making the rounds of the room, sniffing at each toy and knocking over the Green Army Men. They were helpless to defend themselves.

Andy's mother came in, carrying a wicker dog bed and two bowls that said DOGGY.

"I'm not sure this is the best idea," she said, "having

Buster sleep with you."

"He'll be good, I promise," said Andy.

"Any problems with him and he goes

back to the laundry porch."

Andy put the dog in the

basket and said, "Stay!" But the

minute he left the room, the puppy raced after him.

"The puppy's going to ruin Andy's room!" said

Woody. "And who knows what he'll do to us! This calls

for drastic action."

"All we have to do is teach the little fella some

manners before he has a chance to rip us to pieces," said Buzz. "Or, I can just fire my laser at him."

"That's it, Buzz!" said Woody. "The part about teaching the puppy some manners. We can help Buster find his way to obedience school."

They gathered in a circle to plan their strategy. "We need to figure out the bad things a puppy would do," said Woody. "Then we'll help him do them."

"How about spilling his food and water?" said RC Car. "I can do that in one run."

"I can dent the furniture," said Buzz. "Make it look like the puppy chewed it."

"We all can help mess up the room," said Bo Peep.

They quickly set about putting the room in complete disarray.

They no sooner got

themselves strewn across the floor than the puppy came

bounding in. *Whap! Zip! Zap!* Sure enough, he took each

toy into his mouth, shook it violently, and tossed it. The

air rained soldiers, dolls, and stuffed animals. The toys

got the puppy into such a frenzy that he skidded about

the room chewing
everything in
sight.

Whiz! RC Car
headed for the
food and water

bowls. Buzz flew at the puppy, who had Rex in his mouth.

Andy's mother heard a crash and came into the room. "Oh, dear!" she said. "I knew it."

Andy spent Christmas night mopping up the mess and placing each toy on its proper shelf. At bedtime he pleaded with his mother, "What fun is a puppy if you can't sleep with it?"

"You have Woody and Buzz," she said.

"They aren't soft and warm," said Andy. He stayed awake listening to his puppy's cries. When he finally drifted off to sleep, a single tear fell down his cheek.

The toys spent a miserable night. Between Andy's being upset and the puppy's whines from the laundry porch, they got no rest. Woody, who loved Andy dearly, could not bear to think he had made

the boy so unhappy.

The next morning, Woody gathered the toys for a meeting.  "Hey, guys. Maybe we were a little hasty. I, for one, don't want Andy to be unhappy. After all, our whole reason for being is to make Andy smile."

"But what if the puppy chews us?" said Rex.

"If you all stay on the shelf where you belong," said Woody, "the puppy can't reach you. Only Buzz and I, here on the bed, are in danger."

The toys behaved themselves and stayed on their shelves. When Andy forgot to put one away, somehow it managed to get back to its safe place.

Andy's mother remarked how neat he was keeping his room and how well Buster was behaving.

"Maybe then," said Andy, "you'll give Buster and me another chance."

And she did.

Each night, snuggled next to the puppy, Woody wondered if his days were numbered, if one morning at sunrise, he and the dog would have a showdown. He liked to think he'd be brave. He would give his all for Andy's happiness.

But that day never came. The first time the puppy nosed Woody, Andy rapped the dog gently across the muzzle. "No, Buster!"

Before long, the toys befriended the dog, who was not vicious, and they realized he was just young and in need of training. That was soon taken over by RC Car, Buzz, and the Green Army Men.

But no one felt as close to Buster as cowboy Woody.